Lo que aprendo / The Things I Learn

Aprendo de mi maestro
I Learn from My Teacher

Robert M. Hamilton

traducido por / translated by
Charlotte Bockman

ilustrado por / illustrated by
Anita Morra

PowerKiDS
press.

New York

Published in 2017 by The Rosen Publishing Group, Inc.
29 East 21st Street, New York, NY 10010

First Edition

Managing Editor: Nathalie Beullens-Maoui
Editor: Sarah Machajewski
Book Design: Michael Flynn
Spanish Translator: Charlotte Bockman
Illustrator: Anita Morra

Library of Congress Cataloging-in-Publication Data

Names: Hamilton, Robert M., 1987- author.
Title: I learn from my teacher = Aprendo de mi maestro / Robert M. Hamilton.
Description: New York : PowerKids Press, 2016. | Series: The things I learn = Lo que aprendo | In English and Spanish.
Identifiers: ISBN 9781499424256 (library bound)
Subjects: LCSH: Learning–Juvenile literature.
Classification: LCC LB1060 .H3455 2016 | DDC 370.15/23–dc23

Manufactured in the United States of America

CPSIA Compliance Information: Batch #BS16PK: For Further Information contact Rosen Publishing, New York, New York at 1-800-237-9932

Contenido

Contents

¡Me encanta aprender cosas
nuevas en la escuela!

I love learning new things at school!

5

Aprendo cosas de mi maestro en la escuela.

I learn from my teacher at school.

Su nombre es el señor Díaz.

His name is Mr. Díaz.

Tengo muchos amigos en mi clase.

I have a lot of friends in my class.

El señor Díaz nos enseña cosas nuevas.

Mr. Díaz teaches all of us new things.

9

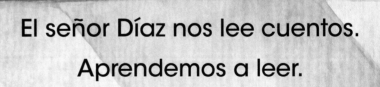

El señor Díaz nos lee cuentos.
Aprendemos a leer.

Mr. Díaz reads stories to us.
We learn to read.

También aprendo matemáticas en la escuela.

I learn math in school, too.

¡Me gustan las matemáticas!

I like math!

El señor Díaz me enseña a escribir los números.

Mr. Díaz helps me learn to write numbers.

15

También me enseña
a escribir las letras.

He helps me learn to
write letters, too.

16

¡Puedo escribir mi nombre!

I can write my name!

Es importante saber escuchar.

Listening is important.

El señor Díaz nos enseña cómo escuchar bien.

I learn from Mr. Díaz how to be a good listener.

También aprendo a levantar la mano
si tengo una pregunta.

I also learn to raise my hand if I have a question.

¡Hago muchas preguntas! El señor Díaz dice que esa es la mejor forma de aprender.

I ask a lot of questions! Mr. Díaz says that's the best way to learn.

Palabras que debes aprender
Words to Know

(la) clase
class

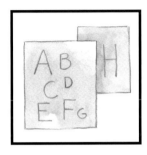

(las) letras
letters

(los) números
numbers

Índice / Index